Amy HODGEPODGE

HAPPY BIRTHDAY TO ME

BY KIM WAYANS & KEVIN KNOTTS

ILLUSTRATED BY SOO JEONG

Grosset & Dunlap

For Elvira, Howell, Billie, and Ivan.
And for Sylvia—the best teacher ever.

GROSSET & DUNLAP
Published by the Penguin Group
Penguin Group (USA) Inc., 375 Hudson Street, New York, New York 10014, USA
Penguin Group (Canada), 90 Eglinton Avenue East, Suite 700, Toronto, Ontario
M4P 2Y3, Canada (a division of Pearson Penguin Canada Inc.)
Penguin Books Ltd., 80 Strand, London WC2R 0RL, England
Penguin Group Ireland, 25 St. Stephen's Green, Dublin 2, Ireland
(a division of Penguin Books Ltd.)
Penguin Group (Australia), 250 Camberwell Road, Camberwell, Victoria 3124, Australia
(a division of Pearson Australia Group Pty. Ltd.)
Penguin Books India Pvt. Ltd., 11 Community Centre, Panchsheel Park,
New Delhi—110 017, India
Penguin Group (NZ), 67 Apollo Drive, Rosedale, North Shore 0632, New Zealand
(a division of Pearson New Zealand Ltd.)
Penguin Books (South Africa) (Pty.) Ltd., 24 Sturdee Avenue,
Rosebank, Johannesburg 2196, South Africa

Penguin Books Ltd., Registered Offices:
80 Strand, London WC2R 0RL, England

Chapter 1

The smell of pancakes and the feel of my dog, Giggles, licking my face woke me up on Saturday morning. "Only six more days until my tenth birthday," I told Giggles, and gave him a pat on the head. "Can you believe it?"

I got out of bed and went over to my wall calendar. I crossed off another day, just like I had been doing all month. Now my birthday was less than a week away!

I pulled out my scrapbook and looked at the page I had made for my ninth birthday. There was a photo of me in front of my birthday cake with my parents and grandparents standing around me. It had been nice, but it was like every other birthday I'd ever had—quiet. There weren't any other kids in the photo.

My Ninth ♡ Birthday

The birthday card I got from my parents last year.

Make a wish!

My grandparents got me two of the best books!

That's because I'd been homeschooled my whole life and didn't know many other kids.

This year, I wanted my birthday to be different. My family and I had moved to Maple Heights not that long ago, and I was going to a regular school for the first time. It had been hard in the beginning, but I had made friends. And this year, I wanted to invite some of them to a sleepover party. But first, I had to ask my parents' permission. I was kind of nervous about what they would say because I'd never asked for anything like that before. But today was the day. I definitely couldn't wait any longer to ask.

"Amy, breakfast is ready. Come on down," called my mom from downstairs.

"Come on, Giggles," I said as I closed my scrapbook. "Let's go get some breakfast . . . and see what my parents think about me having a sleepover."

When I got downstairs, my father, my mother, and her parents were already sitting at the dining room table. My grandparents—the Lims—have lived with us for as long as I can remember.

I sat down and put a stack of pancakes on my plate. After I spread on the butter and poured on the syrup, I said, "You know, next Friday is a very special day."

"Is it Groundhog Day already?" asked my dad.

"Nope," I said sadly. Had he really forgotten about my birthday?

"Is it Presidents' Day?" my mother asked. Could this really be happening?

"No . . ," I said.

"Is it Earth Day?" asked my grandfather. Oh, no! Not my grandfather, too!

"No, but it rhymes with Earth Day," I said, trying to give them a hint.

Everyone was quiet for a moment. Then my grandmother said, "We know what day it is, Little Mitsukai. It's your birthday!"

My grandmother always calls me Little

Mitsukai—that means "Little Angel" in Japanese. She's from Japan, but my grandfather is from Korea.

Everyone laughed, and my dad gave me a kiss on the forehead. They had only been teasing.

"What do you want to do for your birthday this year?" my mom asked. "Should we make your favorite dinner and rent movies?"

What my mom had suggested sounded nice . . . but also really quiet. If I wanted to try something new this year, I'd just have to take a deep breath and ask for it.

"Um, can I have a sleepover birthday party and invite my new friends from school?" I asked.

My parents looked at each other. Then they smiled.

"Of course," my mom said. "It'll be your first slumber party."

"Yay!" I said, practically jumping out of my seat. I couldn't believe how quickly my parents had said yes. If I had known it would be this easy, I would have asked weeks ago. "I'll invite Lola and Pia and Jesse and Maya—"

My dog, Giggles, barked.

"—And of course you, Giggles," I said, petting his honey brown fur.

"What will you girls do at the party?" asked my grandfather.

"Well, I can guarantee they *won't* be sleeping," Dad teased again.

"I want my party to be the best ever!" I said. "I want to do stuff that my friends have never done before."

"Why don't you have a Japanese tea ceremony and wear your kimono for them?" suggested my grandmother.

A kimono is a special type of clothing from Japan. It looks like a robe because it's long and has wide sleeves. You also wear a wide belt around your waist that ties in a special way in the back.

In the old days in Japan, everyone wore

kimonos. Now women mostly wear them on special occasions.

"Do you think they'd like that?" I asked.

"Of course," she said with a big smile. "It will help make your party very special."

"Great!" I said. "I can't wait!"

I had another good idea for my party when Mom and I were clearing the table. "We could do origami, too!" I said.

"Your friends will enjoy that," said Mom with a smile. "I'll take you to Pam's Paper Store to buy the paper tomorrow."

Origami is really cool. It's from Japan, and it's the art of folding paper into beautiful things like birds and flowers. My grandmother taught my mom, and then she taught me. I couldn't wait to show my friends how to do it, because it was part of my family background!

But there's more to my background than being Japanese. My last name is Hodges, but my new friends' nickname for me is Amy Hodgepodge because my family is sort of a hodgepodge. Like

I said, my mom's mother is from Japan and my mom's father is from Korea. My dad's mother is African American and my dad's father is Caucasian. I love that a little part of my parents' and grandparents' looks are all mixed up in me. None of them look alike, but I look like *all* of them!

Some of my new friends' families are mixed, too. Like Lola and her twin brother, Cole—their mom is African American and their dad is Caucasian. And Jesse—she's Puerto Rican and African American. And Pia—she's Chinese and Caucasian. Showing my friends origami and a tea ceremony would be showing them a part of who I am. And there's no one like me!

That night, I turned on the radio in my room and got to work planning my very first birthday sleepover. I made a list of the snacks I would serve. I'd have stuff like pretzels and potato chips and my favorite snack, double chocolate chip cookies.

Next, I had to think about the invitations. I wanted them to be really special—something my friends would keep even after the party. I pulled out a big box from under my bed and started looking through my paper scraps. Suddenly, I got a great idea! I drew a little pattern, and then I traced it onto some paper.

As I worked, I sang along to Amber Skye. She's my favorite singer. She has an awesome voice! I was singing "Friends Are Forever" so loudly that I didn't hear Mom come into my room to say good night.

When Mom tapped me on the shoulder, I nearly jumped.

"Look, Mom!" I said. "I'm making envelopes for my invitations that look like little kimonos!"

"Oh," said Mom, smiling. "They're beautiful. And each one is different! You're putting a lot of work into each one."

"Thanks, Mom," I said with a big smile. "I can't wait for my sleepover!"

Before I fell asleep that night, I reached

for my scrapbook. I love scrapbooking—it's
been one of my favorite hobbies since my
grandmother gave me some pretty handmade
paper. Ever since then, I've filled up my
scrapbook with photos, letters, and little
keepsakes of all my fun times. Like the stub of
my plane ticket when we flew to Hawaii and a

picture of Giggles dressed up in a top hat and tuxedo for Halloween. (I think he's still mad at me for that one!)

I took another look at the photo from my ninth birthday party. This year, my birthday was going to be awesome! I couldn't wait to scrapbook it with birthday cards, scraps of wrapping paper, and tons of photos of my new friends and me. I fell asleep that night thinking about my party, with all of us laughing, painting our toenails, and hanging out in our pj's.

Chapter 2

On Sunday morning, I got to do one of my favorite things—hang out in Lola and Cole's tree house. It's in their backyard, and you need to go up a wooden ladder painted in rainbow colors to get into it. Their dad built it for them. His job is to design houses, so this wasn't just a tiny shack. No way! It was huge—with windows and doors and a cool slanted roof!

"Hi, Amy!" Lola called down as I came into the yard. "Come on up! Maya just got here."

I loved hanging out inside the tree house, and today it looked better than ever! It had bright blue carpeting all over. And each wall was painted a different color—pale orange, pale green, pale yellow, and light blue. And there were even curtains in bright blue fabric!

"Wow!" I said.

"It's finally finished!" said Lola excitedly. "We painted it and put in the carpet last weekend."

"Isn't it the *coolest*?" asked Maya.

"I want to live here!" I giggled, kneeling down to run my hand over the smooth carpet. "And now there's a table," I said. I sat on the floor and crossed my legs under the new low wooden table. "Hey, it's perfect!"

"Have a snack!" said Lola, pointing at a plate of apple slices, cheese, and crackers.

"Are Pia and Jesse still coming over?" I asked Lola. Even though Jesse and Maya had Mrs. Musgrove as a teacher and the rest of us had Mrs. Clark, we all were studying Alaska in social studies class. We'd planned on studying for the quiz that we were going to have on Monday, and I was going to surprise everyone with my party invitations afterward.

Lola looked out the window. "Oh, here they come. Come on up, you guys!" she called.

Pia and Jesse were just as amazed at the tree house's new look as we were. Lola happily told her story all over again as we ate our snacks.

"Okay, enough with the chitchat," said Jesse. She was always ready to get to work. "Who knows the capital of Alaska?"

Lola quieted down and opened her textbook.

"Um, Juneau?" I asked.

"Right!" said Jesse. "Now you get to ask a question, Amy." Studying with friends,

especially in a tree house, made schoolwork a
lot more fun!

After about an hour, we all felt that we were
ready for the quiz, so we put away our books.

"I have a surprise for everyone," I said
excitedly, opening up my backpack. Finally, I
could hand out my party invitations!

"Ooh, what's this?" asked Lola as I handed
her a small, fat, pink "kimono" envelope. It had
tiny gold foil cutout flowers glued on it.

"Open it!" I said, smiling.

"How cute!" said Lola, admiring the envelope
and turning it over. "It looks like a tiny little robe."

"It's a kimono, actually," I said. I watched
Lola pull out a small piece of colorful paper. I'd
made a tiny origami bird—a crane—and glued
it to the paper.

"It's so pretty!" squealed Lola. "Hey, it's an
invitation to your birthday slumber party . . .
this Friday night. I can definitely come! It's
not like I'll be going to the Amber Skye concert

that night, anyway."

"Amber Skye concert?" I asked.

"Yeah, she's coming to town," Lola replied. "I got an e-mail about it because I'm the president of the Amber Skye Fan Club in Maple Heights. But the tickets sold out really fast, and we couldn't get any."

"Well, at least you can come to my party now!" I smiled really big and handed an envelope to Jesse. "Here you go," I said. I thought hers had turned out the best. I'd even glued on silver ribbon to make the *obi*, or sash.

"It's almost too pretty to open! You made this whole thing *yourself*?" Jesse asked, running her finger over the envelope.

"Uh-huh," I said as I handed Pia and Maya their invitations. Suddenly, I felt a little shy. But it felt good to know how to make something no one had ever seen before.

"I'm going to put it above my bed," declared Maya, holding her red kimono envelope up in the air.

"This is amazing!" cried Pia, looking closely at her own invitation.

"It's gonna be so much fun," I promised them. "I hope it'll be the coolest birthday party you ever went to!"

"Really?" asked Maya. "My cousin Jolie's fourteenth birthday party was pretty cool. There was a deejay. Well, it was actually my older cousin Tommy—"

"This should be better," I said. "Because you're going to see things—and do things—and maybe even wear some things you've never seen, or done, or worn before!"

"Wear something I've never worn before?" cried Pia. "I can't wait for that!" Pia loved clothes. Today she was wearing a striped sweater dress, sparkly pink tights, and shiny white boots. I couldn't wait to let her try on my kimono and show her the special sandals I wear with it. She was going to love that.

Luckily, everyone said they were pretty sure they could come but would ask their parents first. And they seemed really excited about it.

This was the kind of thing I'd hoped would happen once I stopped being homeschooled and started fourth grade at Emerson Charter School. It had been scary doing something new and going to a place where I didn't know anyone. But sometimes you have to take a chance and do something you've never done before. I was so glad I did! If I hadn't, I wouldn't have been sitting in such a cool tree house. Or planning my big party!

Chapter 3

That afternoon, something happened that made all my excitement fade. It all started when the phone rang.

"I'll get it!" I called.

"Okay!" Mom called back. She was in the basement.

As usual, Giggles ran ahead of me to the desk—sometimes I think he wishes *he* could answer the phone.

"Hello?" I said.

"Mr. Hodges, please! This is Sam Keller," said a man with a booming voice.

"Oh, he's not here right now," I said, reaching for a pencil. "May I take a message?"

"Sure," he said. "I'm just checking in with him about the move to California."

Move to California?! My stomach did a flip-flop.

"Um—" I said, dropping the pencil. *What move to California?* We were moving? Again? Why hadn't anyone told me?

"Er, hello?" said the man after a moment. "Can you ask him to call me back later? I'd appreciate it." He was speaking so loudly that I felt like my eardrum was going to burst!

"S-sure, Mister Yeller," I said, trying to grab the pencil as it rolled around on the floor. "I mean Mister, um—"

"Keller," said the man. "It's *K-e-l-l-e-r*. Thank you."

"Sorry! Okay, I'll tell him. You're welcome. Bye," I said.

As I stuck the note to the fridge with a magnet, I could feel tears filling up my eyes. We'd only been in Maple Heights for a little while and I was just starting to make friends. Could we really be moving? How could my parents do this to me?

Maybe Mr. Keller called for a different reason, I told myself . . . something that didn't have anything to do with us moving. But what? I couldn't think of anything that made sense.

I ran upstairs and flopped on my bed.

"Amy, are you ready to go to Pam's?" Mom called from downstairs a few minutes later.

I'd forgotten that we'd planned to go to Pam's Paper Store for the origami supplies!

"Uh, I'll be right there," I said. I looked in the mirror and wiped my eyes. Then I slowly went downstairs.

Mom was on the phone when I came into the kitchen.

". . . Yes, that's right," she was saying. "I'll need the biggest boxes you have . . . can you deliver them next week? . . . Thursday will be fine . . . Thanks. Bye."

Oh, no, I thought. Why would Mom order boxes—big boxes? I could only think of one reason.

"Um, there's a note for Dad on the fridge," I said. I wanted to see if Mom would talk to me about us moving.

"Thanks, sweetie! Let's go," she said, reaching for her purse.

She wasn't acting like she was keeping a secret, but I was too chicken to ask her about what was happening. I decided I'd wait until later.

As I put on my seat belt, my mind was going

a million miles an hour. As Mom started the car, I got an idea. I'd point out cool things about Maple Heights to Mom as we drove around! Maybe it would help to remind her about why we'd moved to Maple Heights in the first place.

"I think I'll get the car washed on the way to Pam's," said Mom, turning into Whale of a Wash.

"Oh, I love the whale on the sign," I said, looking at my mom. She just smiled. "They could have used a rat or a weasel or a skunk, but instead they chose a cute little whale," I continued.

Soon it was our turn to go through. The smell of soap came into the car. "Ah. That's the best smell in the whole world. I just love it!" I said. "Don't you, Mom?"

"It's not bad," Mom said. But she didn't seem to care that much. Maybe she was thinking about moving to California instead.

"Wow! What an amazing car wash!" I cried as the big brushes came down. "So cool. Isn't it, Mom?"

"Er—yes, I guess so," said Mom.

"It's newer than the one where we used to live," I pointed out. "See? There are *lots* more brushes. Our car will be even *cleaner* here! Everyone will think it's brand-new!"

Mom laughed. "Well, all right," she said. "That's a good thing." Mom gave me a funny look. I guess I was overdoing it.

Pam's was just a block away from the car wash. It was a small store, and today it was pretty crowded. "Amy, I'll meet you in the origami section," said Mom. "I just want to go find some tape."

As I headed to the back of the store, I had to squeeze past someone. As I said, "Excuse me," I realized it was Jennifer Higgins. *Oh, boy,* I thought.

Jennifer was one of the prettiest girls at school, but also the meanest. She'd made fun of my dress on my first day of school this year, but that wasn't the worst part—she'd made fun of me because of how I look, too. She'd said I looked weird! Luckily, Lola, Pia, and Jesse were with me then, and they made me feel better. It turned out that Jennifer had made fun of them before, for the same reason—because they were from mixed families.

"Oh, *hi*, Amy," she said without a smile. "What are you doing here?"

"Hi, Jennifer," I said. "I'm just buying some stuff for my birthday party."

"Party?" she asked. "*My* birthday's coming up, too. Guess what Liza, Gracie, and I are doing? We're going to see Amber Skye in concert. My dad got us front-row seats—the most expensive tickets you can get!"

Oh, boy, I thought again.

Just then, my mom came back. She smiled at Jennifer. "Hello," she said. "I'm Amy's mom."

"Oh, *hi!*" said Jennifer. She gave my mom a huge smile. "I'm Jennifer Higgins! It's so nice to meet you, Mrs. Hodges."

Wow! I couldn't believe Jennifer was being so nice. I'd never seen her like this.

"Thank you, Jennifer," said my mom. I could tell she was impressed with Jennifer's good manners. My mom was big on manners. "Are you in Amy's class?"

"Oh, yes," said Jennifer. "We're in Mrs. Clark's class together." She smiled again at my mom. "Well, I have to go find my mom. Byeee!"

She did a cute little wave to my mom and walked away.

"Bye, Jennifer," said my mom with a smile. She turned to me. "What a nice girl. You're so lucky to have such nice kids in your class, Amy."

Jennifer's a big phony-baloney! I wanted to say. But that wouldn't make any sense to my mom. Besides, maybe this was a good thing! I smiled and said, "I really am lucky, Mom. I love the kids in my class! And I love my school! I sure would miss it if I left!"

"I'm sure you would, sweetie," said Mom, but she was busy looking at origami paper, so I couldn't see her face to get a clue about what she was thinking.

I guess I should thank Jennifer for that, I thought as we stood in the checkout line. *Maybe she just helped make my mom want to stay in Maple Heights!*

That night at dinner was the first time that

I wasn't hungry for Obaasan's yummy homemade miso soup. Mostly I just sat there and watched everyone's face for some hint about us moving, but no one did or said anything strange. I wanted to just come out and ask, but every time I tried, the question got stuck in my throat.

"What's the matter, Little Mitsukai?" asked my grandmother. "Don't you feel well?"

"You're really quiet tonight, Amy," said my dad. "That's not like you."

"Maybe she is thinking very important thoughts," said my grandfather with a smile.

"Oh, I feel fine!" I said as I forced down a spoonful of soup. "So, um, how was everyone's day today?"

"Fine," said everyone around the table, nodding.

Maybe if I show them how much I love my new school, they won't make me leave, I thought.

"You'll never guess what we learned about in school last week," I said with a big fake smile. "We learned all about global warming!

And greenhouse gases! It's so important that everyone knows a lot about that and that we all try to help the Earth! 'Cause if we don't, it's just gonna get hotter and hotter!" I barely took a breath. Suddenly, I just couldn't stop talking. "Oh! And I got to play the guitar in music class—it's really hard—but it's fun! And oh, yeah, I can't believe I almost forgot—I'm finally learning how to play soccer and it's great! I'm not good—yet—but I think I will be if I keep trying! Emerson Charter School is awesome. I lo-o-o-o-ove it!"

Everyone smiled.

"That's nice, sweetie," said Mom. But Mom's voice sounded far away, like she was thinking about something else. *Like what? Moving?* I wondered.

"Hey, what's for dessert?" Dad asked Mom with a big smile. "Maybe some—brownies?"

Mom smiled and shook her head. "You know, honey, I can't find Bonnie's Organic Brownie Mix anywhere! I don't see why Super Foods doesn't carry it—it was so popular back home."

"That's a shame," said Dad sadly. Those brownies are his favorite. "But what about Gibson's Supermarket? Or the health food store?"

"I've checked them all, honey," said Mom, shaking her head. She turned to me. "I guess Amy and I could make brownies from scratch after dinner. How about it, sweetie?"

"Uh, maybe tomorrow, Mom. May I please be excused?" I asked. I just couldn't sit there another minute. I felt like I was going to explode. If we were going to move, why was no one talking about it?

Chapter 4

Monday morning didn't start off very well.

"It's time to get up already?" I asked Giggles, who was whining—he always whines when the alarm goes off. I was so tired! All night, I'd been thinking about how awful it would be to move. But at least I'd come up with some ideas about how to change my parents' minds.

After breakfast, just as I was leaving for the bus stop, I felt like I was forgetting something . . .

"My reading homework!" I said, suddenly remembering. I ran up to my room to look for it.

By the time I found it under my scrapbook,

I had to run as fast as I could to the bus stop. The last kid was getting on the bus when I turned the corner.

"Wait!" I called. Thankfully, the bus driver heard me and held the door open. I ran even faster and tripped. Luckily, I caught myself before I fell flat on my face—with everyone on the bus watching me from the windows!

My face was hot and I was breathing hard when I stepped in. I was so embarrassed to see a blur of faces staring at me.

"Did you have a nice *trip*?" wisecracked a boy. It was Rory, the same kid who'd played a mean prank on me on my first day of school.

"Amy Hodgepodge!" shouted my friends from the middle of the bus. As I walked past Rory, I just ignored him.

"See you next *fall*!" he shouted.

Lola waved to me. I was glad she wasn't sitting next to anyone. I plopped down next to her. "Whew!" I said. I turned around and waved to Pia, Maya, Jesse, and Cole.

"You made it!" said Lola, putting her arm around my shoulders.

"I'm really tired," I said. "I didn't get much sleep." I sighed and looked out the window.

Lola nudged me. "Why not?" she asked.

"Yeah, why not?" shouted Jesse over the hand-clapping game that Pia and Maya were playing.

"Well," I said slowly, "I think my family is— moving to California."

"What!" cried Lola and Jesse.

Pia and Maya stopped clapping.

"But you just got here," protested Maya.

"Yeah, you can't move again!" said Cole. "When are you leaving?"

"I don't know," I said. "Um, my parents haven't really said anything about it yet."

"Then how do you know you're moving?" asked Jesse.

I told my friends about the phone call from Mr. Keller and the boxes that Mom had ordered.

"There might be other reasons for those things," Jesse pointed out. "You never know—"

"Well, if you are moving," Pia cut in. "I hope your parents will change their minds." She put her hand on my shoulder.

"That's what I'm hoping, too," I told my friends. "I'm thinking of how *I* can change their minds. Can you all help me write a letter today at lunch?"

"Sure!" said everyone.

It made me feel good to know that my new friends would be sad if I moved. Soon they all began to talk about other things, but Lola seemed to know, more than the other kids, how sad I was. "Don't worry, Amy," she said in a low voice. "Maybe you won't move. And if you do, well, I'll ask my parents to put me on a plane and I'll come visit you!"

"Thanks, Lola," I said. I had to smile, thinking about Lola flying by herself all the way to California to see me!

All too soon, the bus pulled into the school.

Suddenly, I had butterflies in my stomach. I just didn't feel ready for school that day. I went straight to my class, sat down at my desk, and pretended to read a library book while I waited for Rusty. I had to ask him to do a favor for me.

Finally, Rusty came into the classroom. He was a good friend of Cole's and now mine, too. He was always making us laugh, even though his life wasn't very easy.

"Hi, Rusty! You live near Super Foods, right?" I asked.

"Yup!" said Rusty. He was trying to juggle three striped rubber balls.

"If I write a letter to the store, would you be able to drop it off for me?"

"A letter to the store? You mean, like, to the manager? Sure," said Rusty as he kept juggling. "Why are you writing a letter to the store—is it something for school? Anyway, my mom's probably going there today. I usually have to help her."

Just then, Mrs. Clark came to my desk.

"Amy, did you feed the fish today? It's your turn, you know," she said.

"Whoops," I said, jumping out of my seat. I'd forgotten! "Sorry, Mrs. Clark!" My face turned hot—again. I had to hurry and feed the hungry fish while Mrs. Clark took attendance. Then it was time for history—and the quiz that my friends and I had studied for over the weekend. I'm sure I did okay on the quiz, but in between each question, I couldn't stop thinking about how awful it would be to move out of Maple Heights.

After history, we went down the hall to the music room. Music is one of my favorite classes. I love to sing, and some people say I'm pretty good at it. I even sang lead in this year's school talent show. I was really nervous about it, but the performance turned out great!

"Good morning, class," said Mr. Ship, our music teacher, playing a few notes on the piano.

"Good morning, Mr. Ship," everyone said.

"Let's begin by warming up our voices," said Mr. Ship. "Sing with me—do, re, mi, fa, so, la, ti, do!"

"Do, re, mi . . ." I sang, but not as loudly today. I couldn't stop thinking about how awful it would be to get ready to move . . . to pack our things all over again . . . and then unpack the boxes in a new place. That was a lot of work. I'd have to go to a new bus stop again and stand there with kids I didn't know . . . maybe they wouldn't be very nice . . . and maybe I wouldn't like my new school as much as Emerson . . .

"Earth to Amy!" cracked Jackie Bailey in a loud voice. When I heard my name, my daydreaming ended! The class giggled.

I looked at Mr. Ship. "Er, yes, Mr. Ship?" I asked. My cheeks were burning. Mr. Ship smiled. "I just asked if you'd like to play the tambourine while we sing," he said.

"Oh! Okay," I said. I was so embarrassed that I looked down at the tambourine in my hand for the rest of the class.

Finally, music class ended and it was time for lunch. Now I could just think about the stuff *I* wanted to think about—like getting my parents to stay in Maple Heights.

"Oh, no! Guess who's sitting at our table," said Lola as my friends and I walked into the noisy cafeteria. I looked over to where we all sat every day. Jennifer Higgins and her friends Liza and Gracie were there.

"They never sit there," said Rusty.

"I'll bet they took our table just to bug us," said Jesse.

"Well, there's nowhere for our whole gang to sit except at the table next to them," Pia pointed out.

So Lola, Maya, Jesse, Pia, Rusty, Cole, and I sat down and pretended not to notice them and started to eat and talk.

"Hey, Lola," said Jennifer in a loud voice, looking at Lola's Amber Skye T-shirt. "That's a nice T-shirt. Are you planning to go to Amber

Skye's concert on Friday night?"

Oh, boy, here it comes, I thought.

"Uh, no," said Lola.

"Why not?" asked Jennifer with a giggle.

"Yeah, why not?" echoed Gracie. "Aren't you, like, supposed to be her number-one fan?"

Lola looked down at her sandwich. "My mom couldn't get tickets," she said. "They sold out too fast, but I'll be at Amy's birthday party that night, anyway."

Jennifer, Liza, and Gracie giggled.

"Well," said Jennifer, "that's too bad. But can you believe it? *We're* going. For my birthday. Front-row seats!" The three girls high-fived one another and laughed loudly.

Lola's face turned red. "Ooh," she said to us in a low voice. "She makes me so mad!"

"And guess what else!" said Jennifer, looking at all of us. "We also have backstage passes to meet Amber Skye after the show! Can you believe it? There's going to be a party backstage, and *we'll be there!*"

"We'll be there! We'll be there!" chanted
Gracie and Liza.

"We'll be there! We'll be there!" mocked Lola.
"I wish they were there right now."

My friends and I tried not to look at them. We
were so mad! But we tried not to show it.

"Just ignore them," I said in a low voice to
Lola. "Remember? That's what you told me to do
on my first day of school."

"I know," said Lola. "But it's hard sometimes."

By now, Jennifer, Liza, and Gracie were laughing so hard that they could hardly eat their lunch.

"Maybe Amber Skye will ask Jennifer to go on tour with her," Cole snickered.

"And take her far, far away," added Rusty. We all laughed.

"Let's go," Pia said, standing up. She turned to Jennifer's table. In a supersweet voice, she said, "We'd really love to hear more about it from the Maple Heights Braggers Club, but we're going to the library now. You know, I don't think that boy all the way in the corner heard about you going to the concert. Maybe you can ask the principal if you can announce it over the PA system!" Pia flipped her hair and then started to walk away. "Let's go, everybody."

Wow! I wish I could have done something like that. Pia was awesome!

So we all got up and left. I couldn't help looking back at Jennifer's table. They were still laughing and high-fiving. Now I wanted more than anything to make sure that my party was the best ever.

"That was a good idea to get out of there and go to the library," I told Pia as we walked down the hall.

"Those girls are so obnoxious," said Jesse, scowling.

The library seemed extra quiet compared to the cafeteria. We all sat down at a long table near the windows.

"Okay, everyone!" I said. "I have to write a letter to Super Foods. Can you help me? We only have a few minutes left before the bell rings."

"Super Foods?" everyone asked in surprise. Everyone except Rusty.

"Why are you writing to the store?" asked Jesse.

"To get them to sell Bonnie's Organic Brownies," I explained. "We had them back home, and we love them. They're so-o-o good! But they don't have them here. It's something

that my parents don't like about Maple
Heights! So, it's one of the things I thought
about last night when I couldn't sleep—"

"Oh, I get it," said Maya. "You're going to try
to get the store to hurry up and get it so your
parents will like Maple Heights more."

"I know! Why don't you make it sound like
your mother wrote the note?" asked Jesse.

"Yeah!" said Pia. "That's perfect, 'cause the
store might not pay attention to a kid's letter."

"You're right," I said, pulling a pen out of my
backpack. Jesse always had such good ideas!
Dear Super Foods, I began to write. *My name is
Soo Lim Hodges . . .*

With my friends' help, I wrote my letter.

Dear Super Foods,

*My name is Soo Lim Hodges. My family
just moved here from the Midwest. Back there,
we made brownies every Friday night with
Bonnie's Organic Brownie Mix. But now we just
sit around and feel really sad on Friday nights,
because we can't find this brand at your store.*

These brownies are so amazingly chocolaty, and aren't bad for you at all. The mix has no wheat, dairy, nuts, or other things that some people are allergic to. But my family and I love it just because the brownies taste so amazingly good! Please put Bonnie's Organic Brownie Mix on the shelves right away or my family might go CRAZY!

Thank you,

Soo Lim Hodges

P.S. It would be really cool if you would put Bonnie's Organic Waffle Mix on the shelves, too. They are waffley-icious!

"Perfect!" Lola said after I read the letter out loud. "It doesn't sound like a kid wrote it."

"Yeah, it's really good," added Cole.

"Thanks for helping me!" I said, smiling at my friends.

Rusty reached for the note. "I'll drop it off," he said with a smile.

"Thanks, Rusty," I said. "I hope this works!"

As my friends started talking about other

things, I sat back in my seat and looked out the library window. What else could I do to make Mom and Dad fall in love with Maple Heights and keep us from moving? I had to think fast.

Chapter 5

The next morning, I got up a little early to do some scrapbooking before school.

"Hi, Dad," I said when I came downstairs. I didn't see Dad much in the mornings. He usually went to the hospital before I got up.

"Oh, that Sparky," muttered Dad. He was coming in from getting the newspaper. "Er, good morning, honey."

"What about Sparky?" I asked. Sparky is the dog next door. He's a pug, and he's really round and cute.

"Sparky is a *bad* little dog," said Dad. "Every morning, it's the same thing. He takes my newspaper and hides it in the bushes or drags it through the wet grass. So then I have to put shoes on, go outside, find it, and read a soggy

paper—every morning." He tried to separate
the paper's torn, wet pages, muttering, "Why
did we have to move next door to a newspaper
thief?"

Yikes! I thought. *One more thing to make
my parents not like Maple Heights!*

During school that day, it was kind of hard
to keep my mind on my work. I was thinking
about how I could help my dad with the Sparky
problem—without my dad knowing.

Lunchtime in the cafeteria that day wasn't
so bad—Jennifer and her friends had gone back
to their regular table.

"I guess Jennifer thinks she was mean
enough to last awhile," said Lola with a laugh
as we all sat down at our table.

"Hey, Amy," said Rusty. "I dropped that note
off at Super Foods."

"Thanks a lot, Rusty," I said. As I pulled
out my lunch, I looked around the table at
my friends. "Guess what! Now I have a new

problem—Sparky the Newspaper Thief!"

"Sparky? Who's Sparky?" asked Pia with a giggle.

I told my friends about my dad's problem with the bad little pug.

"What are you going to do?" asked Jesse.

"I'll have to get up extra early tomorrow so I can get the paper before Sparky does!" I replied.

"You'd better go to bed extra early, too," said Rusty with a chuckle.

"I know," I said with a sigh. "I know."

That afternoon I had a dentist appointment. As Mom and I were driving there, a big dark cloud came up out of nowhere. Soon it began to rain really hard.

"Oh, no! So much for our nice clean car," said Mom sadly, turning on the windshield wipers. "Sometimes I wish we lived in California. Wouldn't year-round sunshine be nice?"

I thought fast. "But there are earthquakes

in California," I said. "Really bad ones! And mudslides and wildfires. And sometimes it doesn't rain enough there so they can't put out the fires. But we'll never have that problem in Maple Heights. What a *relief*! Good ol' Maple Heights."

"Well, that's true," said Mom with a chuckle. "We get *plenty* of rain here. And I'm sure we'll get plenty of snow, too."

That went pretty well, I thought as I sat back in my seat. *Maybe I can still manage to change my parents' minds about moving.*

❀ ❀ ❀

"Is that you, Amy?" called my grandmother when we got home from the dentist.

"It's me, Obaasan!" I said, heading upstairs to my grandparents' room.

I loved their room. It was almost like an apartment! Their bedroom was big, and so was their super-fancy bathroom. They also had a sitting room next to it with a sofa, a chair, a big footstool, and a TV. A door led to their very

❀ 51 ❀

own balcony. I loved reading out there with the beautiful flower boxes and hanging plants. It was my favorite part of the house. Except for my room, of course.

"I don't have any cavities," I announced, hugging my grandmother. Then I noticed what she'd been doing.

"Obaasan! You have the *dōgu* out," I said.

"Just getting ready," said my grandmother.
"I haven't seen these things since we moved."

Dōgu is the Japanese word for the tea
ceremony utensils, like the tea caddy and
the bowl that the guests drink from. My
grandmother's *dōgu* were very old—they had
belonged to her grandmother. I carefully picked
up the pretty tea scoop, which was made of
bamboo, and hugged my grandmother. "Thank
you for doing this for my party, Obaasan," I
said.

A Japanese tea ceremony is a big deal. You
have to practice for years before you know
how to do it right. My grandmother began to
learn when she was young. What makes the
ceremony special is that everything happens in
a certain way and at a certain time. Everything
has to be just right.

One of the first things that happens during a
tea ceremony is that the host (my grandmother)
cleans the tea bowl, a whisk, and the tea scoop

with a special cloth. She does this in a special order in front of the guests. Next, she puts green tea in the bowl and adds hot water. Then she whisks the tea. Even this is done in a certain way.

Next, she serves the bowl to the guest of honor (at my party, that would be me). The guest of honor bows to the host and then to the next guest. Then the guest of honor raises the bowl to the host. It's a sign of respect to her.

By the end, all the guests have sipped from the bowl. They turn the bowl so that each person drinks from the clean place on the bowl. Finally, it's given back to the host, and she cleans everything again, in a certain way. She bows to the guests, and that's the end of the ceremony. Sometimes a tea ceremony can go on for five hours! But ours would be shortened for my party. It would be about half an hour long. We had special Japanese music to play during the whole thing. My grandmother was planning on arranging flowers in a beautiful Japanese style for the ceremony, too.

I hoped my friends were going to love it.

Suddenly, I cheered up. I was still really worried about moving—but seeing my party starting to become real, with the big bags of snacks, the *dōgu* out, and the kimonos out of their box made me want to call Lola right then to talk about it.

Lola answered the phone on the first ring.

"Hello?" she cried. She sounded really excited about something. And extra-extra happy!

"Hi, Lola, it's Amy!" I said.

"Oh! Amy. Um, hi." Lola sounded really surprised that it was me. "Uh . . . er . . . I thought you were going to be Maya," she went on. "I've been waiting for her to call me back."

"Oh," I said. "Well, I just called to say hi. I'm getting ready for my party—"

"Oh!" Lola cut in. "That's the other line. I'll—uh—call you back. Bye."

"Er—okay, bye," I said, but Lola had already

hung up the telephone.

I sat there for a minute, trying to figure out what had just happened. Was I making things up, or had Lola not been happy to hear from me? And why was it so important for her to talk to Maya right now, anyway?

Oh, well, Lola said she'd call me back. She'd probably fill me in on what was so important. So I went back down the hall to be with my grandmother. But an hour later, Lola hadn't called back yet.

And by the time I had to get ready for bed, she still hadn't called.

After Mom and Dad said good night, I lay in the dark and petted Giggles, who was making funny little snoring sounds. But even with Giggles there, I felt so alone. And my room seemed extra dark.

Why would Lola act so weird to me and then not call me back? I must have done something wrong. But what?

Great, I thought. *One more thing that's*

going wrong in my life.

Why did everything have to be so weird now?

Why couldn't everything stay perfect? Just for a little while?

Chapter 6

When my alarm clock went off Wednesday morning, it was really dark outside. It seemed like I'd just gone to bed.

"Shhh!" I whispered to Giggles, who of course was whining. "We can't wake anyone up." *Oh, boy,* I thought. This whole trying-to-get-my-parents-to-not-leave-Maple Heights thing was becoming a lot of work!

"Stay here, Giggles," I ordered as I got out of bed. I threw my Emerson School sweatshirt over my pj's, stepped into my plastic clogs, and sneaked downstairs. When I got to the front door, I peeked out the window. Good! The paper was there. Sparky wasn't up yet!

Eeeeeeee! The door creaked when I opened it. I hoped my mom and dad didn't hear that.

But just as I was quietly closing the door behind me, Sparky appeared!

"Nice Sparky," I said, leaning down to get

the paper. "Good boy . . ."

But Sparky was not a good boy. He grabbed the paper and ran.

"Wait!" I shouted. I took off after Sparky. He sure could run fast! But I was catching up!

Then I tripped, and my shoe fell off.

Oof! I fell down, hard. Then, when I tried to get up, I slipped on the wet grass and slid into a bush.

Ow! A branch scratched my face. But I got up and finally caught up to Sparky! I grabbed the paper—but he didn't let go.

"Good boy," I said as Sparky growled and shook his head back and forth. "Give it to me." Finally, I got both hands on the paper and just pulled. I pulled so hard that—*splat!* I fell into a cold puddle of water! When I sat up, I realized that I only had half of the paper! Sparky was sitting there watching me, breathing hard, with the other half of the paper still in his mouth.

Then he took off.

That's when I gave up and stumbled home

with my half of the paper. Two jogging ladies gave me a funny look as I walked back to my house.

Of course, it was just my luck. Dad opened the front door, looking for the paper.

"Amy! What are you—oh, that Sparky!" Dad shouted.

Without saying anything, I handed him the soggy paper and went upstairs. *California, here we come,* I thought sadly.

Dad was still home when I came downstairs in my school clothes. He chuckled and gave me a big hug and a kiss on the top of my head. "Let's take care of that scratch on your face," he said, leading me to the kitchen for some ointment. "Does it hurt?"

"No," I said. "It's not a big deal."

I felt like such a klutz. Two falls in one week!

"I guess it's time for me to talk to Sparky's owners," he said. "But not right now. After we get you fixed up, I'm driving you to school. But before *that*, we'll stop for a special breakfast at Billie's Café—because it was really sweet of you to get up so early to help me! You didn't need to do that."

Oh, yes, I did! I thought. *Dad, please don't make us move!*

I almost said it out loud. Why couldn't I just ask why we had to move? Because I was a great big chicken. And because I knew my family wouldn't talk about anything else once we started. That's what happened the last time we moved.

I ran up the stairs to say good-bye to Mom, who was just getting dressed. My grandparents weren't up yet.

"Have a good day, sweetie," said Mom as she hugged me. She ran her finger over my bandage. "We'll talk later about everything, okay?"

I hope that means my adventure with Sparky, I thought. *Not moving.*

Chapter 7

It was fun having breakfast with Dad at Billie's Café, but it made me a few minutes late for school and I didn't get a chance to talk to any of my friends before I got to class.

Later, when I got to the cafeteria for lunch, my friends were already at our table with their heads close together, talking. They all had really serious looks on their faces. Since I hadn't gotten to talk to any of them before school, I wondered what was up.

"So what are we gonna do?" Maya was asking.

"Hey, everyone!" I said, throwing my backpack down on a chair. Everyone looked up, and Maya clapped her hand over her mouth.

What were they just talking about? I

wondered. *And why did they stop when I got here?*

"Oh! Hi, Amy," said Maya.

"Amy!" cried Jesse when I sat down.

"What happened to your face?" asked Lola.

"Yeah, what happened to your face?" asked Maya.

"Is that why you weren't on the bus today?"

asked Pia, looking worried.

Suddenly, I felt a little bit better. Maybe nothing weird was going on. Maybe my friends had just been talking about what to give me for my birthday!

"Well," I said, "this morning I got up really early. I had to stop Sparky the Newspaper Thief!" I told my friends the whole story, and by the end, I was laughing about it as much as they were. "At least I got a trip to Billie's Café out of it," I said.

It felt good to laugh. But still, something seemed different. Everyone got really quiet after my story, and Lola never said she was sorry for not calling me back.

"I'm starved. I hope my mom packed sushi for me today!" I said, opening my backpack.

Pia didn't ask for a tiny piece as she usually did.

After a while, I couldn't take it anymore. "What's up?" I finally asked. "You all seem worried or something."

The girls looked at one another. They looked like they'd been caught doing something wrong.

"Uh," said Lola, looking down at her lunch. "I guess I'm just thinking about my schoolwork . . . Wow! This turkey sandwich is soooo awesome!"

"You have a turkey sandwich almost every day," I teased her. "Why is it better today?"

"Um, I guess it's the, uh, different kind of mustard my mom bought?"

"Really?" I asked. "You can tell stuff like that?"

Everyone was quiet for the rest of lunch. The worst part was that no one really looked at me and they all still had that guilty look.

I started feeling a little upset. My lunch seemed to stick in my throat. *What's going on?* I thought. *It's almost like my friends were talking about me behind my back. But why? Don't they like me anymore?*

I was glad to get out of there when the bell rang to end lunch. I wondered what it was going to be like with my friends that afternoon on the bus ride home. I couldn't stand it if they were still acting weird to me.

It turned out that Lola and Jesse weren't on the bus, but Pia and Maya sat in the back together and talked in low voices. So I just read my book a few seats away from them. Actually, I didn't read that much. Mostly I just sat there and stared at the page and wondered why my whole life felt different than last week. *I've got enough to worry about already without problems with my friends,* I thought sadly.

After school, I took a long walk with my grandparents. We used to do that every day when I was homeschooled. We loved looking at the different kinds of flowers in the neighborhood, going to the museum, and reading in the park. I missed doing that stuff with them. Now that I was in school, I didn't have as much time for that.

"Maple Heights sure has a lot of pretty

flowers," I said as we came to a house with a colorful garden.

"Yes, it does!" said my grandfather. He stopped to look at a yellow rose and put his arm around my grandmother. "There are more beautiful flowers here than in our last neighborhood."

At least they seem happy here in Maple Heights, I thought. *Maybe that makes three of us.*

"Is everything all right, Amy?" asked my grandfather. He smiled at me. "You have been very serious lately."

It's hard to hide anything from Grandfather, I thought.

I wanted to hug both my grandparents and ask them about the move. I wanted to ask them why my friends were suddenly being so weird.

But I didn't. I just put on my big fake smile and said, "Everything's fine, Harabujy. I'm just thinking about schoolwork. That's all."

Harabujy means "grandfather" in Korean.

After all, my grandparents couldn't tell me why my friends were acting so strange. And if we were moving, I didn't really want to find out there, on the street.

That night, every time the phone rang, I thought it might be Lola. But it wasn't.

When I went to bed that night, I remembered that my grandmother had once told me that thinking happy thoughts before falling asleep would bring me good dreams.

Everything will be better soon, I told myself. *And my party will be the best party my friends ever went to. And we'll all have a great time together.*

Please.

Chapter 8

The next morning, the sky was extra dark. It was pouring rain.

I don't care, I thought as I threw the covers back and got out of bed. *I don't care that it's a rainy day. I'm just gonna be happy today. And not worry about my friends. Or when my parents are finally going to talk about the move. I'm just going to think about my party— after all, it's tomorrow!*

Just thinking about my party and crossing off the last day on the calendar before my birthday made me feel a lot better! So did my mom telling me at breakfast that she'd give me a ride to school so that I wouldn't have to wait for the bus in the rain.

There was so much traffic on the way to school that I was almost late. I wouldn't get to talk to my friends until lunchtime.

In the cafeteria that day, Rusty was testing out his newest silly gadget—a big fake nose with a mustache that curled up at the ends.

"Listen to someone who *knows* what he's talking about," said Rusty.

We all cracked up as he pointed to his fake nose and then twirled the ends of his mustache.

It was great to be laughing with my friends again. But no one was talking about my party, and it was tomorrow! Something still seemed to be wrong. But I just didn't know what!

After school, I ran to catch up with Lola and Jesse. They were walking toward the bus. I thought I heard Lola say, "Amy's party," but I wasn't sure. Finally, someone was talking about my party and how awesome it was going to be.

"Hi!" I called, running up to them.

"Oh, hi, Amy," said Lola. She looked nervously at Jesse.

Then both the girls looked away from me.

That was all I could take. I decided to finally just ask them what was going on. "What's up?" I asked. "Why are you all acting so weird?"

Lola stopped walking. "Listen, Amy," she said.

"A-hem." Jesse cleared her throat and looked at Lola.

"What?" I looked from Lola to Jesse.

Lola took a deep breath. "Um, you know how I'm the president of the Maple Heights chapter of the Amber Skye Fan Club?"

"Uh-huh," I said. Why did I have butterflies in my stomach all of a sudden? I was getting the feeling I was going to hear some bad news—but I couldn't figure out what.

"Well," Lola went on, "you know how Amber Skye's concert is tomorrow, and my mom couldn't get tickets—"

"Uh-huh," I said.

"But then the funniest thing happened," Jesse blurted out. "Lola's mom got a phone call from a lady who works for Amber Skye, and—"

"Yeah!" Lola cut in. "It was so amazing! She gave me free tickets and backstage passes for after the concert so we could meet Amber Skye!"

Jesse cleared her throat again. Both girls

watched my face anxiously.

"Oh," I said, realizing that if they went to the concert, they'd miss my party! Even though I thought I was going to cry, I made sure to smile. My big fat fake smile.

"That's okay," I went on. "I know you're a huge fan of Amber Skye. You should go!" I was trying to act like nothing was wrong, but my voice came out kind of squeaky.

"Really? Oh, thanks! Um, so, did I say that I got five tickets? Well, anyway, yeah . . . I got five free tickets. So—Jesse, and Maya, and Pia, and me are *all* going," added Lola. "With my mom. We were going to get a ticket for you, too, but we figured you wouldn't want to miss your own party."

My cheeks began to burn. For a second, I couldn't breathe.

"Oh! All of you," I said. "Um, don't worry, there's a bunch of other girls coming to the party. Have a great time at the concert!" I laughed so they'd think everything was fine.

"Oh, good. What a relief! Who else is coming?" asked Jesse.

"Oh, you know—a bunch of girls," I said.

"Like who?" asked Jesse.

Yikes. No one else had been invited! What could I say now? But luckily, Lola changed the subject before I could answer.

"You're the best, Amy," she said. "Thanks for,

you know, understanding! We'll get you a T-shirt at the concert."

"Your party is gonna be so awesome, Amy. I want to hear all about it," said Jesse.

"And *I* want to hear all about the concert!" I said with another big fake smile.

But all I *really* wanted was to get out of there before I started crying.

As I walked toward the bus, I began to think about everything. How excited I had been about the tea ceremony, the expensive origami paper I'd spent time picking out, the kimonos that I'd finally unpacked, and the special invitations I'd made.

All of my work. All of my plans. For nothing.

My first birthday sleepover party was over, and it hadn't even happened yet.

Chapter 9

The bus ride home was not fun. My friends talked about the stupid concert the whole time—even Rusty and Cole, and they weren't even going! I had to act like it didn't bother me, so I just kept smiling my fake smile until my cheeks hurt. I wished I could just draw on a smile and keep it there.

I was glad to say good-bye to everyone, but I didn't want to go home, either.

How could I tell my mom what had happened? If my family saw I didn't have any friends coming to my party, it would be even harder for me to get them to stay in Maple Heights— Bonnie's Brownies or not.

"Hi, sweetie! Why don't we run over to Miss Goobles?" asked Mom as soon as I walked in the door. "We still haven't gotten the double chocolate chip cookies for your party."

Here we go, I thought. *I have to get this over with.*

"Uh—" I said. I took a deep breath. "Mom, I've changed my mind. I, um, just want a family party—not a sleepover. No friends."

"Really?" asked Mom, blinking. Mom always blinks a lot when she's surprised. "But it's tomorrow, and your friends said they were coming. Are you sure that this is what you want to do?"

"I'm sure," I said in a small voice. I just couldn't face telling Mom about what had happened with Lola and Jesse. It hurt too much even to think about it.

"Well—did you and your friends have an argument?"

"No."

"Then why aren't they coming to the party?"

Oh, Mom! I wanted to cry out. *Help. My party's ruined. And I don't want to move!*

I wanted to tell her everything that had
happened. But instead, I just looked down at the
floor and tried not to cry.

"Hmm," said Mom softly. "Well. All right, then, sweetheart, if that's what you really want."

Mom only calls me "sweetheart" when she knows I'm upset.

I headed upstairs to my room. All I wanted to do was cuddle with Giggles on my bed for the rest of the night. I didn't want to talk to anyone.

"We'll have pizza and cake then—just us! Okay?" called Mom cheerfully up the stairs. "Sweetheart?"

"That sounds nice," I called back, trying to sound like I meant it.

Chapter 10

Friday came. My birthday.

I'd never felt sad on my birthday before. But of course, I had to pretend like I wasn't.

At breakfast, Mom said, "Amy, how about if I pick you up at lunch today and take you to the Tick Tock Diner for a birthday lunch?"

"Hey, thanks, Mom!" I said. "That would be fun!"

What a good idea! This way, I wouldn't have to face my friends at lunch.

When I saw my friends at school, they all wished me a happy birthday and gave me hugs, but I couldn't wait to get to my seat and take out my notebook. I was worried that they'd ask me again who was coming to my party—*and* I didn't want to hear any more about how awesome that stupid concert was going to be.

I was glad to leave school to have lunch with my mom, but even that didn't cheer me up. My mom could definitely tell that something was wrong. I'd never been so down on my birthday before. She did her best to make me feel better—she even ordered me a special milk shake for dessert. But I was going to need way more than a milk shake to feel better about my party getting ruined *and* about moving.

At school, I pretty much kept to myself for the afternoon, doing whatever I could to not have to talk to my friends. I ducked into the bathroom when I saw Lola and Maya walking toward me in the hallway. Another time, I bent down to retie my shoelace (even though it wasn't even untied) to avoid talking to Pia and Jesse.

At the end of the day, I didn't sit with any of my friends on the bus ride home. I'd walked really slowly to the bus so that I'd have to sit in the front, far away from them.

"Have a great party, Amy!" said Lola as we all got off at the bus stop.

"Yeah, have fun!" chimed in the other girls.

"Thanks, have fun at the concert," I said with one last big fat fake smile before I took off.

"It is your special day, Amy," said my grandmother when I got home. She put my hands in hers. "I think we must still dress for the occasion. We will wear our kimonos, all right?"

"All right, Obaasan," I said, squeezing her hands. My grandmother always knows how to make things special for me.

When we got to my grandmother's bedroom, Mom took my kimono off the rack and handed it to me. It was pink, with darker pink butterflies and red blossoms all over it. Mom's was pale green with pink, green, and yellow flowers and with gold thread around one of the flowers. And my grandmother chose her silk midnight blue kimono, with white branches and flowers.

Putting on a kimono takes time.

First we put on white socks, called *tabi*. Next we put on the underclothing. It's called *juban*, and it's a white cotton top and skirt. Then we put on our kimonos with the right side of the kimono over the body and overlapped it with the left side. I adjusted the white collar of the slip to show around my neck, just under the kimono collar.

Then we put on our *obi* belts. Mine was red. This took a while, but when we were finished, I felt like a different person.

"Very nice!" said my grandmother as we looked at ourselves in the mirror.

"May I come in?" asked Dad as we put on our *zori* sandals. "The pizza's here! And I want to take a picture."

When we posed for the photo, I started feeling a little bit better. Still, I couldn't help feeling sad that my birthday had turned out differently than I had hoped it would.

Ding-dong! Ding-dong-ding-dong-ding-dong-ding!

"Who could that be?" I asked. After all, it wasn't like I was expecting anyone. Whoever it was sure liked ringing doorbells.

I carefully went downstairs to answer the door, trying not to trip in my kimono. Kelly, my cute little four-year-old neighbor, was standing there, wearing a frilly pink dress, white tights, and shiny black mary janes. Her bright red hair had been curled, and she had a fake diamond

tiara on her head. She was holding a present and a card. Kelly thinks I am the coolest "big kid" in the world.

"Ooh, pretty!" she cried, touching my kimono. "Happy birthday, Amy! Your mommy told me." She handed me the present. "Here! We went to the mall, and we bought this for you. It's a book for you about a girl and she has a horsey and—"

"Oh! Thanks, Kelly," I said. As sad as I was, I had to giggle. "But you're not supposed to say what the present is, you know."

"Okay," said Kelly, skipping past me into the living room. "Hi!" she called to my family. "Ooh! Pretty!" she said again when she saw my mom and grandmother in their kimonos.

"Hi, Kelly," said Mom. "You look very nice." She turned to me. "Honey, I forgot to tell you that I invited Kelly. You know how she loves you."

This is just great, I thought. *I'm the only kid at Emerson with four-year-olds at her birthday party.*

"You're just in time for food, Kelly!" said Dad as he opened up the pizza box.

"Yum!" squealed Kelly. "And look at all your presents, Amy." She picked up one of my gifts and shook it hard. "Can I open it?" she asked in an extra-sweet voice.

Just then, the doorbell rang again.

"Who could it be?" asked my grandfather, looking confused.

"Perhaps a mystery guest," said my grandmother, smiling.

Probably another four-year-old, I thought, opening the door.

It was Rusty and Cole!

"Happy birthday, Amy!" they shouted.

"Wow! You look so cool!" said Rusty, looking at my kimono. "We were just biking around, and we thought we'd say hi. And get some snacks!" He laughed.

"You get your birthday punches now," kidded Cole. He pretended to punch my arm really hard. "One, two, three, four, five—"

"Come on in," I said. "Um, we were just going to have some pizza."

"Cool!" said Cole. "Hi, everyone!" he called as he walked in.

"Hi, Cole," called my family. "Hi, Rusty!"

Cole turned around to look at me. "Where is everyone?"

"Yeah," said Rusty, who was following me.

"I thought you were having a bunch of friends over. Other than Lola, Pia, Jesse, and Maya, I mean—"

"Uh—" I began.

My family looked confused. After all, they still didn't even know why I had changed my party to a family party!

What was I going to tell Cole? That I hadn't really invited other people?

And what should I say to my family?

I wanted to hide.

"There weren't any other friends—" I began. Suddenly, my eyes filled up with tears and I started to cry, right there in front of everyone . . . at my own birthday party.

My family quickly came over to hug me.

"What's the matter?" asked Dad. "Don't cry, honey."

"It's all right," I said. I hiccuped and looked around at everyone. It was time to explain everything.

I turned to Cole. "See, I only invited Lola,

Maya, Jesse, and Pia. They're, uh, the only girls I know well enough to invite to a sleepover party."

Then I turned to my family. "But they're all at the Amber Skye concert. They got tickets at the last minute, and so I said they should go . . . that I'd invited other people—"

I started crying all over again, even though everybody was staring at me. I just couldn't help it.

"Oh," said Rusty and Cole at the same time. They looked down at the floor.

"I just told them I had other friends coming so they wouldn't feel bad about missing my party. Don't tell them I was crying, okay?" I asked the boys. "It's not a big deal."

"But it *is* a big deal," said Rusty. "You made a lot of plans. And you're all dressed up." He looked kind of bummed. So did Cole.

"Would you like to have some pizza with us?" Mom asked them.

"Sure," said Rusty.

"Okay, thanks," said Cole. Just after he answered my mom, he took out his phone and started sending a text message.

I was glad the boys were staying, even though I was so embarrassed that they saw me cry. But at least it was beginning to feel more like a party.

"Pizza! Presents! Pizza! Presents!" chanted Kelly.

"I'll be right back," I told everyone. I just needed to be by myself for a minute. So I went to the bathroom, blew my nose, splashed some water on my face, and took a deep breath. Then I went back out and opened my presents.

My mom and my grandmother always make my gifts really beautiful. They use pretty paper and cut out flower shapes and make little tags with tiny origami. They're always so pretty that I almost hate to open them.

After that, we all played a few party games and then had our pizza. Mom was just beginning to cut the cake when—

Ding-dong! Ding-dong!

"Who could it be *now*?" I asked. I trudged to the door.

Chapter 11

I almost fell over when I opened the door. Lola, Pia, Maya, and Jesse were standing there!

"Happy birthday, Amy!" they all shouted, hugging me. "Wow! Look at you! You look sooo cool!"

I didn't know what to say!

"How—how—is the concert over already?" I asked.

"No!" said Lola. "But Cole texted our mom—"

"It was almost intermission!" interrupted Jesse. "And Lola's mom read the message and it said—"

"That we were the only friends you'd invited to your party," Maya cut in.

"We decided that it was more important to

be here for your party than to see the rest of the concert . . ." added Pia.

"Even Amber Skye's concert!" finished Lola. "So here we are—*ta da!*"

"Wow," I said. "I can't believe you left the concert to be with me on my birthday." I was so excited that I had such great friends. *They must really care about me,* I thought.

"Well, aren't you gonna let us in?" asked Jesse. "Let's get this party started, everybody!"

"Can we watch the rest of the concert on TV?"

asked Pia as my family and friends greeted one
another. Giggles and Kelly were so excited that
they kept jumping up and down together.

"Sure," said Dad. He grabbed the remote and
found the right channel. He turned the volume
up loud so we could feel like we were at the
concert, in the front row!

Soon my friends were chowing down on pizza
and cake and dancing to the music. Even my
grandmother and grandfather were having fun
watching the concert and talking to my friends.

My grandmother squeezed my arm. "See?
Mystery guests," she said with a chuckle.

"You're right, Obaasan," I said. And then I had
to say it. I had to get it off my chest. "Oh, Mom
and Dad, I don't want to move! Can't we just stay
in Maple Heights? I have such great friends—"

"Move?" asked Dad.

"Yeah! Please don't move, Mr. and Mrs.
Hodges!" cried all my friends.

Mom started blinking.

"Are we moving?" cried my grandfather. He

looked at my grandmother.

"I'm not going anywhere," said my grandmother. She frowned and folded her arms over her chest.

"Me neither," said Kelly. "Can I have another piece of cake?"

"So, we're not moving?" I was still confused. Mom was still blinking.

"We're not moving, everyone!" said Dad, laughing.

"YOU'RE NOT MOVING?" they all shouted in unison.

"But what about the phone call?" I asked Dad. It was still hard for me to believe what he'd just said.

"What phone call?"

"You know—Mr. Yeller, I mean Keller. He called about moving to California. *Remember?*"

"Oh, that. Sam Keller is a fellow doctor who needed me to give him some pointers about a hospital in California, that's all. *He's* moving."

"YOU'RE NOT MOVING!" screamed Lola,

Jesse, Pia, and Maya, jumping up and down. The boys gave me a high five.

"But—what about all the boxes you ordered?" I asked as my friends hugged me. "And, well— sometimes it just seems like you don't like it here."

Mom and Dad smiled.

"The boxes are for storing things in the attic," Mom explained. "And—well, you know how it's been a big adjustment for you to live in Maple Heights and go to Emerson?" asked Mom. "Well, it's been a big change for us, too."

"We're older," said Dad with a chuckle. "So it's even harder for us to do things in a different way—or to live with different weather!"

"Well, I love Maple Heights," said my grandfather. He smiled at my grandmother and poured her some tea.

"Me too, Harabujy," I said, hugging him.

"Hooray! I'm not moving!" As soon as I heard myself say that, I felt a million pounds lighter. Now it was my turn to jump up and down—

even if it was pretty hard to do in a kimono!

"Oh! I almost forgot," said Lola, pulling a little bag out of her backpack and handing it to me. "These are just souvenirs. We'll give you your real presents tomorrow."

"Yeah," said Maya. "We didn't want to waste any more time going home and picking up your gifts."

Inside was a baby blue T-shirt that said Amber Skye and Amber Skye's brand-new CD!

"Wow, thanks, everyone," I said. This time, my big smile was one hundred percent real!

Lola put her hand on my shoulder. "Amy, if we'd known that we were the only ones lucky enough to be invited to your birthday party, we would've never gone to the concert."

"Thanks," I said. "I—I should have told you the truth about everything." I looked at all my friends. "Thanks for giving up the rest of the concert for me," I said.

"No problem," said Pia. "We never should have kept a secret from you. Anyway, Amber Skye will be back next year. And next time, you're coming with us!"

"Oh!" said Jesse, practically dropping her slice of pizza. "We forgot to tell you! When we were walking out of the arena, we ran into Jennifer and Liza and Gracie! They hadn't even gone in yet! And Jennifer was freaking out—"

"She'd lost their tickets!" Maya cut in. "She was crying—and Gracie and Liza looked really mad!"

"So did Jennifer's dad," added Pia, giggling.

When I followed my mom into the kitchen to refill some glasses, she gave me a big hug. "Amy, sweetie," she said. "You really need to talk to us when you're upset about things."

"I know," I said into her shoulder. I was thinking about all those crazy things I did to make my parents want to stay in Maple Heights. And how upset and sad I'd been—for nothing! "I'm never going to do anything like that ever *again*!"

"Good!" said my mom. "And as for the party, if you'd just told me your friends got tickets to the concert, we could've moved it to another night. That's all."

"I know, Mom," I said. "I was so upset. I just didn't think about that."

"*That's* why you need to come talk to us as soon as you're upset about anything," said Mom, smoothing down my hair. "We love you and we'll help you."

"I will, Mom," I said. "I promise."

"So, do you still want to have your sleepover with the tea ceremony?" asked Mom. "We can reschedule it."

"Can we, Mom?"

"Of course!"

I hugged Mom again. "Thanks, Mom. I love you."

Just then, the phone rang, and Mom answered it.

"Hello?" she said. "Yes, this is Soo Hodges . . . Who is this? Oh, Super Foods . . ."

Super Foods! They were calling about my letter! I tried not to giggle, but Mom looked

really confused. She started blinking a lot again.

"Yes," said Mom, holding the receiver close to her ear. "You say you're going to start carrying Bonnie's Organic Brownies? Well, that's great . . . er, but—how did you know that I wanted them?

. . . From my letter to the manager . . . Oh . . . well, thank you for calling . . . bye-bye."

As soon as Mom hung up, I started to laugh.

Mom smiled and put her hands on her hips. "Amy, did you have something to do with 'my' letter to the manager?" she asked.

But before I could answer, Pia rushed into the kitchen. "Amy!" she cried. "Amber Skye's singing 'Friends Are Forever'!" Pia and I began to sing along as we hurried back to the living room.

"Friends are forever!
Friends are together
Through good times and bad . . ."
Jesse and Lola joined in:
". . . Happy times and sad,
I'll be there for you . . ."
Finally Maya joined the group:
". . . And all you go through
'Cause friends are friends
From the beginning to the end."
"Aroooo!" barked Giggles.

Everyone cheered. For the rest of the night, we celebrated my birthday . . . and the fact that I'd be staying right where I belonged—in Maple Heights!

Don't we look pretty?

I was so surprised!

My Tenth Birthday!

Me and all my friends!

Kim Wayans and Kevin Knotts are actors and writers (and wife and husband) who live in Los Angeles, California. Kevin was raised on a ranch in Oklahoma, and Kim grew up in the heart of New York City. They were inspired to write the Amy Hodgepodge series by their beautiful nieces and nephews—many of whom are mixed-race children—and by the fact that when you look around the world today, it's more of a hodgepodge than ever.